Baby Animals

By Garth Williams

 A GOLDEN BOOK • NEW YORK

Library of Congress Control Number: 2003109659
ISBN: 0-375-82933-4
www.goldenbooks.com
Printed in the United States of America
First Random House Edition 2004
10 9 8 7 6 5 4

Baby Bear holds his toes. He wants to
be a circus bear when he grows up. He
wants to make all the children laugh.

Baby Squirrel has come to see what his little cousin the chipmunk is so busy doing at the end of the long branch.

Baby Chipmunk has a delicious nut and he is going to stuff it into his cheek before the baby squirrel gets it. They both like nuts to eat.

Baby Fox is full of mischief. He is hoping he will find a sleepy rabbit to chase, but the rabbits are hiding.

Baby Lamb is dancing over the hills
and meadows. It is spring and everyone
wants to dance after the cold winter.

Baby Opossum is pretending to be dead.
If a big bad dog comes along he will play
dead and the dog will go away.

Baby Skunk is fooled by his playmate
lying so still.

Baby Lion roars "Ahrrroum" just like
his father. One day he hopes he will be
king of the jungle.

Baby Tiger says, "You frighten me."
Baby Tiger looks like a great big kitten,
and he loves to play like one.

Baby Giraffe is so tall that he has to bend down to stay in the picture. He never makes a sound, and he can run very fast.

Baby Monkey swings from branch to
branch. He holds on with his two hands,
with his two feet, and with his tail.

Baby Orang-utan also lives in the trees. He is putting a leaf on his head to keep the sun off.

Baby Kangaroo hops like six rabbits. He uses his big tail to keep his balance, so he won't fall.

Baby Koala Bear lives in Australia like
Baby Kangaroo. He sleeps in the
eucalyptus tree at night and eats its leaves
in the daytime.

Baby Woodchuck has been asleep all winter long. Now he is eating tender grass and a small, tasty root. Soon he will be very plump.

Baby Mink has just caught his first fish.
He is going to show it to his mother and
then eat it for breakfast.

Baby Rabbit has hopped away from his
mother's side. His eyes are wide open. He
sees a big bumblebee. "I don't think I will
go any farther," he says.

Baby Racoon washes his apple. He never eats anything until he has washed it first. He even washes a fish.

Baby Camel walks very well and can go for a day without drinking. He keeps food and water in his fat humps.

Baby Owl says, "Whoooooooo's undressed and whooooooo's in bed? Whooooooo's awake and whooooooo's asleep?"